Harry and His Bucket Full of Dinosaurs

Jump into Dino World!

Based on the original Harry stories created by
Ian Whybrow and Adrian Reynolds
Illustrated by Art Mawhinney

PUFFIN BOOKS
Published by the Penguin Group: London, New York,
Australia, Canada, India, Ireland, New Zealand and South Africa
Penguin Books Ltd, Registered Offices: 80 Strand, London WC2R 0RL, England

puffinbooks.com

First published in the USA as *Into the Bucket* by Random House Children's Books 2006
Published in Puffin Books 2007
1 3 5 7 9 10 8 6 4 2

Made and printed in China
ISBN: 978-0-141-50137-6

"Harry, we have to go," Mum called. "We don't want to be late to pick up Nan."

Harry was under the bed. "I'm coming," Harry called back. "I want to wear the cap Nan gave me, but I can't find it."

"Where can it be?" Harry asked his dinosaurs. "I just had it this morning."

"Is it orange?" asked Taury. "With a brown brim? And a yellow H on the front?"

"That's it!" cried Harry. "I've got to find it. I want to wear it when we pick up Nan."

Patsy looked on top of the dresser. *No cap.*

Taury looked under Harry's table. *No cap.*

Harry looked in the wardrobe. *No cap.*
   "We've just got to find it!" said Harry.

Harry heard Sid ask, "What is everyone looking for?"
"My cap," said Harry. "We can't find it anywhere."
"Hmmm," Sid said. "I just saw Trike with it."
"Where was he?" asked Harry. He looked for Sid.
"Hey, Sid, where are you?"

"In Dino World," said Sid. His voice was coming from inside the bucket!

"Where?"

"You know, Dino World . . . ," said Sid's voice again, ". . . in the bucket."

Harry looked over at the bucket. There was a faint glow coming out of it.

The glow was getting brighter.

Harry looked at the dinosaurs. Just then a couple of small stars shot up out of the bucket.

"Wow!" shouted Harry. "I thought the bucket was empty."

"Not really, Harry," Taury answered. "You should take a closer look."

Suddenly Pterence flew up out of the bucket. "Come on, Harry, let's go!" he said. "You're going to love Dino World!" Then he turned round and flew right back into the bucket.

"What's it like there?" called Harry.

"It's called Dino World, isn't it?" laughed Taury. "Imagine how fun and exciting it's going to be. And the only way to get there is to jump!"

"Let's go! . . . On three!"
And they counted together.

"ONE!"
Patsy jumped into the bucket.

"TWO!"
Taury jumped into the bucket.

"THREE!"
And Harry jumped into
the bucket.

"I'm on my way to Dino World!"

"You made it, Harry!" cheered Patsy.
"I knew you'd find it," said Taury.

"Wow!" said Harry. "This is the best place ever."

"It's more fun than a frog on a Ferris wheel," said Patsy.

"But it's so big!" marvelled Harry. "How are we ever going to find Trike and my cap?"

"There are lots of places to look, so let's go," said Taury.

They went to Pepper Rock and there was an amazing cave.

But no Trike.
And no cap.

They went to the edge of the Primordial Swamp and called Trike's name. There was lots of mud.

But no Trike.
And no cap.

Then they went to Rock Lake. The water was blue and cool.

But no Trike.

And no cap.

"Sometimes Trike climbs Pillow Hill. The top is soft and bouncy," Sid explained to Harry. "And even if he isn't there, it's high enough that we might see him."

But when they got there, Trike wasn't at the top of Pillow Hill. In fact, he was nowhere in sight.

"We're never going to find Trike and my cap," sighed Harry. "Dino World is just too big!"

"I have an idea," said Pterence excitedly. He pointed at a little clump of bushes in the distance. "What if we go to the Wishing Well and wish that we could find Trike and the cap?"

"Great plan, Pterence," said Taury.

And they all hurried off.

Soon they were standing beside the Wishing Well.

Harry closed his eyes and began to wish. "I –" Just then Trike walked out of the bushes wearing Harry's cap!

"Trike!" cried all the dinosaurs.

"My cap!" cried Harry.

"Oh, Harry," said Trike. "I thought it was a cap for me . . . it matches my colours perfectly."

"Sorry, Trike," said Harry. "Nan gave it to me. I really want to stay and explore Dino World, but I have to go!"

"That's okay, Harry," said Taury. "There will always be time for Dino World later."

"Mum, I'm coming! I found my cap!"

Harry, Sam and Mum picked Nan up at the store.
Harry was excited to tell her all about Dino World.
He told her about jumping in the bucket. All about the
Primordial Swamp. He told her about the cave at Pepper
Rock. He told her about all of the things he could see
from high up on Pillow Hill.

"Oh, Harry," said Nan. "That is so exciting. Did you make a wish at the Wishing Well?"

"No, I didn't have time . . . ," Harry began. And then he stopped.

"Wait a minute, Nan. I haven't even told you about the Wishing Well yet . . ."

Harry looked at Nan. She was looking out the car window and smiling. Harry wondered, How does Nan know about the Wishing Well in Dino World?